Franklin's Valentines

To good friends, Tarah and Caitlin Blum — S. J.

To Papa Wilf, with love — B.C.

Franklin is a trade mark of Kids Can Press Ltd.

Text copyright © 1998 by P.B. Creations Inc.
Illustrations copyright © 1998 by Brenda Clark Illustrator Inc.
Interior illustrations prepared with the assistance of Shelley Southern.

We acknowledge the support of the Canada Council for the Arts
and the Ontario Arts Council for our publishing program.

Kids Can Press Ltd.
29 Birch Avenue
Toronto, Ontario, Canada
M4V 1E2

Printed in Hong Kong by Wing King Tong Co. Ltd.

CDN PA 98 0 9 8 7 6 5 4 3 2 1

Canadian Cataloguing in Publication Data

Bourgeois, Paulette
    Franklin's valentines

ISBN   1-55074-480-1 (bound)   ISBN 1-55074-482-8 (pbk.)

I. Clark, Brenda.   II. Title.

PS8553.085477F73   1998   jC813'.54   C98-931272-0
PZ7.B68Fr   1998

Franklin's Valentines

Written by Paulette Bourgeois and Sharon Jennings
Illustrated by Brenda Clark

Kids Can Press

FRANKLIN could count to ten and back again. He knew the days of the week, the months of the year and the holidays in every season. Today was Valentine's Day, and Franklin was counting the valentines he'd made for his friends. He wanted to be sure he hadn't forgotten anyone.

"Hurry up, Franklin," said his mother. "You'll miss the school bus!"

Franklin rushed to find his hat and mittens and boots. He tossed his valentines into his bag.

"I'm going!" called Franklin, and he hurried out the door.

At school, Mr. Owl gave the class a valentine spelling bee and valentine arithmetic problems. But everyone was too excited about the Valentine's Day party to think about work.

Franklin whispered to Bear, "I can't believe we have to wait until after lunch to give out our cards."

"I can't believe we have to wait until after lunch for the goodies," Bear whispered back.

At last, it was time for the party.

"You may get your valentines now," said Mr. Owl.

Franklin grabbed his bag and reached inside. He pulled out his hat, and he pulled out his mittens. He pulled out a ball and a scrunched-up piece of homework. Then he held his bag upside down and shook it.

"What's wrong?" asked Bear.

"My valentines! They're gone!" cried Franklin.

After Franklin looked everywhere, Mr. Owl
let him phone home. Franklin waited and
waited while his mother searched.

"I'm so sorry, Franklin," she finally said.
"I found your valentines outside in a puddle
of slush. The cards are ruined."

Franklin blinked away tears. He gave the
phone to Mr. Owl and ran out of the room.

Mr. Owl found Franklin in the cloakroom.

"There you are, Franklin," he said. "Your friends are waiting. We can't start the party without you."

"I don't belong at the party," replied Franklin. "I don't have any valentines to give."

"I know," said Mr. Owl. "Your mother told me what happened. And I told the class."

Franklin moaned. "I guess no one's going to give me a valentine now."

"Hmmm," said Mr. Owl. "If Bear lost his valentines, would you decide not to give him a card?"

"I'd never do that!" exclaimed Franklin. "Bear is my friend."

"Maybe Bear feels the same way about you," replied Mr. Owl.

Franklin thought about that.

"Maybe," he said. He cheered up a little.

Franklin and Mr. Owl went back to the classroom.

Franklin watched as his friends delivered their cards.

As the pile of valentines in front of him grew bigger and bigger, Franklin felt sadder and sadder. There were so many, and he had none to give in return.

He sighed as he opened Bear's card.

"What's wrong, Franklin?" asked Bear. "Don't you like my card?"

"I do! But I feel bad because I don't have one for you," said Franklin.

"Oh that's all right," said Bear. "I don't need a valentine to know you're my friend."

Franklin smiled.

Everyone gathered around as Franklin opened his other cards.

"Mine's a turtle cut-out," said Snail.

"Mine's a turtle poem," said Goose.

"And I made up a turtle riddle," said Fox.

"These are great!" exclaimed Franklin. "I just wish I had my valentines for all of you!"

"I just wish we could start eating all these goodies," replied Bear.

Everybody laughed.

That night, Franklin told his parents about the party.

"It sounds as if you have some very good friends," said Franklin's father.

"I sure do!" agreed Franklin. "Next year, I'm going to make them extra-special valentines!"

"Well, you've got a whole year to get ready," replied his mother.

"I don't know if I can wait a whole year," said Franklin.

The next morning, Franklin's mother found him at his table, writing and drawing and cutting and folding.

"What are you making?" she asked.

"It's a surprise," Franklin answered.

His mother smiled. "Well, hurry up. You'll miss the bus."

But Franklin didn't hurry. He wrapped his
artwork carefully and placed the package in his
bag. He made sure that all the buckles were
done up tight. Then he hugged the bag to his
chest and went out the door.

As soon as Franklin got to school, he opened his package and gave everyone a card.

"What are you doing, Franklin?" asked Beaver. "Valentine's Day was yesterday."

"Oh, these cards aren't for Valentine's Day,"
replied Franklin. "They're for Friendship Day. And
Friendship Day can be any day you want it to be."